The World's First Tooth Fairy...Ever

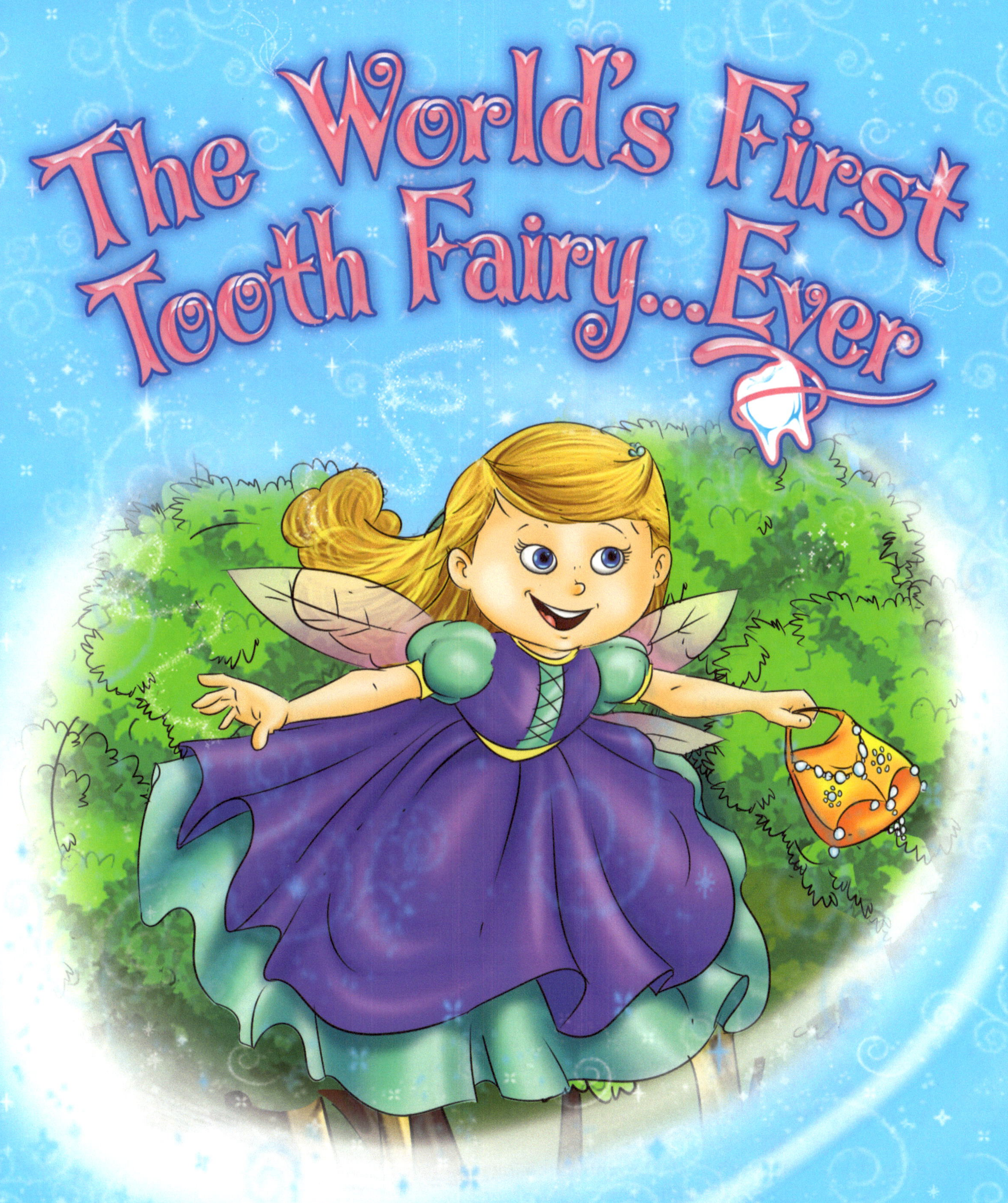

By Zane Carson Carruth

The World's First Tooth Fairy... Ever

The World's First Tooth Fairy…Ever
by Zane Carson Carruth
Copyright © 2016 by Carson Marketing, LLC
All rights reserved. No part of this publication may be reproduced, stored in a
retrieval system or transmitted in any form or by any means, electronic, mechanical,
photocopy, recording, or any other without written permission of the author.
Library of Congress Control Number: 2016919215
Published by Carson Marketing, LLC
www.carsonmarketing.com
Illustrated by BTween Animations
Edited by Jordan Weitz
Prepared for publication by Dimensions Design
Cover design by Roslen Roy Mack

Publisher's Cataloging-In-Publication Data
(Prepared by The Donohue Group, Inc.)

Names: Carruth, Zane Carson, author. | BTween Animations (Firm),
  illustrator.
Title: The world's first tooth fairy ... ever / by Zane Carson Carruth ;
  [illustrated by BTween Animations].
Description: 3rd edition. | Houston, Texas : Carson Marketing, LLC, [2020]
  | Series: The world's first tooth fairy ... ever ; [1] | Interest age level: 003-008. |
  Summary: "Join Abella, a precocious little fairy on her journey through Tulip
  Hollow with her best friend Darcie. Abella finally has the chance to venture out
  of Tulip Hollow and is kidnapped by a big old bee and flown out of Tulip Hollow.
  Find out how Abella frees herself from the bee and discovers children for the first
  time"--Provided by publisher.
Identifiers: ISBN 9780578747224 (hardcover) | ISBN 9781792342936 (softcover)
  | ISBN 9781792347917 (ebook)
Subjects: LCSH: Tooth Fairy (Legendary character)--Juvenile fiction.
  | Kidnapping--Juvenile fiction. | Courage--Juvenile fiction.
  | CYAC: Tooth Fairy--Fiction. | Kidnapping--Fiction. | Courage--Fiction.
Classification: LCC PZ7.1.C4268 Wor 2020 (print) | LCC PZ7.1.C4268 (ebook)
  | DDC [E]--dc23

This book is dedicated
with love and admiration
to my daughter Brittany,
and always and forever
in loving memory
of my son, Chad.

 a land far, far away was a secret world known as Tulip Hollow, where the young fairies played and flew around and had the best time.

All except one...

Abella was a young fairy who was not allowed to venture outside without her parents.

Abella looked outside and sighed. Her daddy walked into her room and said, "What's wrong, Abella?"

"Why can't I play outside with the other fairies, Daddy?" Abella asked.

Her daddy paused for a minute and then said, "Okay, Abella. I suppose you and your friend, Darcie, can fly to the birthday party on Saturday."

Abella woke up very excited Saturday morning. She could not wait to fly to the party!

Smiling and humming, she put on her prettiest party dress. She was ready to get this adventure started!

Abella grabbed her most favorite thing in the whole world: her beautiful orange purse with white pearls all over it.

Abella's mommy reached into the pocket of her dress and pulled out a crisp one-dollar bill and handed it to her daughter. "For good luck," Mommy said.

"Thank you!" Abella said. She wrapped her arms around her mommy and squeezed her tight.

Last, but not least, her mommy put glittery glimmer oil on her wings to make them sparkle.

And Abella and Darcie were off! F*lying is so much fun*, Abella thought.

Buzz, buzz, buzz, buzz.

Abella looked up and saw a big old bee looking at her with mischief in his eyes.

She tried to get away, but that big old bee grabbed her and began to fly in the opposite direction of the party.

"Abella!" She heard Darcie calling, but there was nothing she could do to stop him.

At first Abella was scared, but her wings were tired, and she enjoyed seeing all the flowers below.

After a bit, however, she got bored and wanted to go to the party.

"Mr. Bee, please let me down," she asked nicely.

But the bee kept flying. She asked again, but he held on tightly.

She squirmed, hoping to free herself, but that did not work. She knew what she had to do. She reached up and pinched that mean old bee right in his bee-hind. "Ouch!" he yelled and dropped her!

PLOP! She landed on top of a big pink tulip. "Humph," Abella grunted. "I'm a mess, a terrible mess. I can't go to the party looking like this."

She reached for the hairbrush in her purse when she noticed a white pearl was. The little pearl had fallen off during the wild bee ride.

"My purse is ruined," Abella cried.

Startled by a noise, she looked up. She could not believe her eyes! "Children!" she whispered to herself. Abella had never seen children.

Her daddy had warned her about children. He said,
"Abella, they do odd things. You need to be careful. They
put bugs in jars and poke holes in the lids and stare at
them. And you are tiny enough to be mistaken for a bug."

Abella was curious about the children and flew to an apple tree branch to watch them. They were having a grand time. One of them said, "Let's eat some apples."

"Ouch!" she heard one of the children scream.

What happened? Abella thought curiously. She saw a young boy staring at the palm of his hand.

In the young boy's hand was a tooth. He held it up and grinned, revealing the missing tooth in his smile.

Abella noticed it was white and bright, just like the missing pearl on her purse. Filled with excitement, she knew it would be a perfect replacement. She needed that tooth!

Just then, a woman walked up and said, "Johnny, it's time to go home now."

"Ma! Look, I lost a tooth," he said.

"Yes, you sure did," the mom said, smiling.

Johnny put the tooth into his pocket and Abella wondered if he was going to put that tooth in a jar. Abella followed them, catching a ride on the mom's big floppy hat.

When they made it into the house, Abella hid behind a picture frame to keep an eye on Johnny.

"Guess what I'm going to do with my tooth, Ma?" Johnny asked, jumping around and pulling it out.

"What?" his mom asked.

"I'm going to make you a tooth necklace for your birthday." Abella rolled her eyes and thought, *A tooth necklace... humph.*

"That's sweet, Johnny, but now it's time for a nap," his mom
said.

As they went upstairs, Abella followed silently behind.

Johnny's mom gave him a kiss on the forehead and left.
Abella hid behind a big lamp and saw Johnny slide the tooth
under his pillow for safekeeping.

Abella waited and soon he was sound asleep.

Quietly, she flew to his pillow and slid her hand under it, feeling for the tooth. When she felt it, she smiled and slid it out and put it in her purse. Then she remembered how excited Johnny had been to use the tooth to make his mom a present. He would be sad if she took it.

Abella thought, *I know what I'll do.* She removed the one-dollar bill from her purse and began to slide it under his pillow in exchange for the tooth.

Just then, Johnny's eyes popped open and he saw Abella!

Johnny screamed!
Abella screamed even louder!
She flew as fast as she could out the open window. She
kept going until she was too tired to go any farther.

Abella came to a forest and sat under a tree
to rest and think. She needed to figure out how
to get home to Tulip Hollow.

"Abella," she thought she heard. She looked up and around. "Abella," she heard again.
Then she saw them—Mommy and Daddy and Gage.
"Here I am!" she yelled loudly as she flitted up and down.
They all flew to each other and hugged tightly.

"I am so glad to see you, Mommy and Gage! It's been a crazy day," Abella exclaimed.

"It has been a crazy day, Abella. You can tell us all about it when we get home," her dad said.

They flew back to Tulip Hollow very tired and happy to be back together.

About the Author, *Zane Carson Carruth*

Zane and her husband, Brady, reside in Houston, Texas. She is actively involved in the Houston Grand Opera, Houston SPCA, and the Discovery Green Conservancy. In addition to owning Carson Marketing, LLC, Ms. Carruth is a certified etiquette professional. Both she and her husband are avid thoroughbred horse racing enthusiasts. When not traveling, she cherishes spending time with her three grandchildren, Chloe, Carson, and Truett.

www.carsonmarketing.com
www.etiquettetoexcel.com
www.worldsfirsttoothfairy.com